This book
belongs to:

Hallo X

MESSAGE TO PARENTS

This book is perfect for parents and children to read aloud together. First read the story to your child. When you read it again, run your finger under each line, stopping at each picture for your child to "read." Help your child to figure out the picture. If your child makes a mistake, be encouraging as you say the right word. Point out the written word beneath each picture in the margin on the page. Soon your child will be "reading" aloud with you, and at the same time learning the symbols that stand for words.

Library of Congress Cataloging-in-Publication Data

Schorsch, Kit.
 Jack and the beanstalk / retold by Kit Schorsch : illustrated by Kitty Diamantis.
  p. cm. — (A Read along with me book)
 Summary: Retells in rebus format the classic tale in which a boy finds his fortune at the top of a beanstalk.
 ISBN 0-02-898241-X
 [1. Fairy tales. 2. Folklore—England. 3. Giants—Folklore. 4. Rebuses.] I. Diamantis, Kitty, ill. II. Title. III. Series.
PZ8.S3115Jac 1989
398.2'1'0941—dc19
[E]   89-590
                                                            CIP
                                                            AC

Jack and the Beanstalk

A Read Along With Me Book

Retold by **Kit Schorsch**
Illustrated by **Kitty Diamantes**
Cover by **David Russo**

CHECKERBOARD PRESS
NEW YORK

Jack

mother

cow

Once, long ago, there lived a

poor widow and her only son,

 . Though they were poor,

 and his  earned

enough each day by selling milk

from their 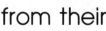 , Milky White.

But the day came when the gave no more milk. Sadly

the widow said to , "You

must take our to market. Be

sure you get a good price for her."

As walked with the

to the market the next day, he

met an old . "Where are

you going?" asked the old .

"To sell my ," said .

"I will give you these **5**

man

5
five

beans

cow

man

hand

Jack

five

colored for your ," said

the old , opening his .

"Ha!" laughed. "A is

worth more than **5** ."

"These are magic ," said

the old . "They will bring

you good luck."

So gave the to the

old and hurried home.

"Did you get a good price for

the ?" asked his when

 got home. proudly

opened his and showed his

 the **5** colored  .

mother

Jack

beans

cow

five

beanstalk

"They're magic!" said .

"Colored !" she cried.

"What will we do? Now we have

no and no money—just 5

old ." And she snatched the

 from and flung them

out the window.

The next morning when

awoke he saw a very large

twisted outside his window.

 hurried outside and quickly

started to climb it. Up, up went

the and up, up went .

At last reached the top.

There he found an enormous

 . At the to the

stood a . "I am very hungry,"

said . "Can you please give

me something to eat?"

castle

door

woman

woman

giant

castle

Jack

"Go away from here," said the . "The wicked who lives in this killed your father and took all his riches. If he finds you, he will kill you too." But begged, so the finally let in.

Suddenly  heard a very

loud thump, thump, thump.

"Quick! Hide in the ," said

the . "If the  finds you

he will surely eat you!"

A moment later the came

in. He sniffed the air and said:

"Fee, fi, fo, fum,

I smell the blood of an Englishman.

Be he alive or be he dead,

I'll grind his to make my ."

oven

bones

bread

woman

food

giant

coins

"Nonsense," said the . "Sit down and eat your ."

After the had eaten he took out a bag of gold and began to count them. But before long he fell asleep.

When saw this, he quickly crept from the , snatched a handful of the gold , and ran away as fast as he could. Down the  and back to his he went. He told her all about the and the .

 and his lived off the gold for some time, but when they were all gone, climbed the  once more.

Jack

oven

beanstalk

mother

castle

| **Jack** |
| **woman** |
| **castle** |
| **door** |
| **boy** |
| **coins** |

 disguised himself so that

the at the would not

know him. knocked once

more at the   .

"Please, could I have something

to eat," he asked the

when she came to the of

the .

"No," said the . "The last

time I fed a he stole some

gold ."

But begged, and finally the   gave him some .

Just then heard thump, thump, thump, thump, thump. The was coming!

food

giant

pot

woman

giant

bones

bread

goose

"Quick! Into this copper ,"

said the . A moment later

the came in and said:

"Fee, fi, fo, fum,

I smell the blood of an Englishman.

Be he alive or be he dead,

I'll grind his to make my :"

"Nonsense," said the . "Sit

down and eat."

When the had eaten he

got out his golden .

"Lay," said the . And

the laid a golden .

As before, the fell asleep.

When saw this, he crept

from the copper .

 snatched the golden

and ran to the . The

called out "Master! Master!"

door

Jack

giant

Jack

beanstalk

mother

axe

The  woke up and ran after

 . But was so quick the

 could not keep up. As

neared the bottom of the

he called to his :

"Bring an  , quick!" As

soon as he reached the ground,

he took the from his

 and struck the as hard

as he could.

Down came the and down

eggs

came the – dead.

 and his lived happily

ever after, rich and happy with

as many golden as they

needed.

Words I can read

☐ axe   ☐ cow   ☐ hand

☐ beans   ☐ door   ☐ Jack

☐ beanstalk   ☐ egg   ☐ man

☐ bones   ☐ eggs   ☐ mother

☐ boy   ☐ five   ☐ oven

☐ bread   ☐ food   ☐ pot

☐ castle   ☐ giant   ☐ woman

☐ coins   ☐ goose